Under the Ground

Written by **Emily Bone**

Illustrated by **Maribel Lechuga**

Designed by Anna Gould and Zoe Wray

Nature consultant: Zoë Simmons
Reading consultant: Alison Kelly

All kinds of creatures live deep under the ground, in dark burrows and caves.

Meerkats sleep and look after babies in their burrows.

2

They come out during the day.

Some meerkats look out for danger.

Others hunt for food.

Scorpion

Bugs dig underground nests or make tunnels through the ground.

Miner bees lay eggs in burrows.

Young beetles are called grubs. They grow up underground.

Earthworms eat rotting roots and leaves.

Young cicadas are called nymphs.
They feed on tree roots.

A nymph digs its way to the surface.

It breaks out of its skin
and becomes an adult.

Then it flies away
to find a partner.

Some birds dig burrows under the ground to lay eggs and raise chicks.

Puffins nest in burrows near the sea. They collect fish to feed to their chicks.

Little penguin chicks grow up inside burrows too.

Burrowing owls sleep in burrows.
They come out during the day.

Young owls stay close
to the burrow.

Adult owls
hunt for food.

Frog

7

Many plants begin their lives as seeds in the ground.

A little shoot grows up. Then bushy leaves grow.

Carrot seed

Root

The carrot begins to grow.

The carrot root grows longer and fatter. It tastes sweet. Bugs eat it.

Slug

9

When a mother fox is going to have babies, she digs a den in the ground.

She gives birth. The babies drink her milk.

Baby foxes are called cubs.

The father fox hunts for food.
He brings it to the mother to eat.

Young rabbit

Fox cubs grow up in the
den. After a month, they
start to explore outside.

Prairie dogs live in burrows. They go
above ground to find plants and
seeds to eat.

They sleep and look after their
young underground.

Mothers stay with their pups.

A prairie dog sees danger.
He barks.

Yip yip!

Hawk

The prairie dogs run into the burrows.
They stay there until the hawk has gone.

Other animals hide underground
from danger too.

Eagle

Squeak!

Pikas squeak to tell other pikas
to return to their burrows.

Skink lizards quickly bury
themselves in soil or sand.

Fox

Rabbits stamp their feet if danger is nearby. Then they run into burrows.

Grrr!

American badgers back into their burrows and growl.

Deserts get very hot. Many animals sleep in cool burrows during the day.

Coyotes leave their burrows at night to look for food.

They howl to tell other coyotes that they're nearby.

Desert tarantulas hunt other
bugs at night.

Kangaroo rats come out of their
burrows to collect seeds to eat.

In some parts of the world it is very cold and snowy.

In a snow storm, Arctic foxes burrow into the snow to stay warm.

Lemmings go from place to place in tunnels they dig under the snow.

A mother polar bear digs a den in the snow at the start of winter.

She gives birth to cubs in the den.

They stay there until the weather warms up in spring.

Some ants live in big underground nests.

A queen ant digs a tunnel.

She lays lots of eggs in the tunnel.
Young ants hatch out of the eggs.

Eggs

Young ants

The young ants grow into adults.
They dig more tunnels.

The ants find food
and bring it back
to the nest.

The queen lays lots
more eggs.

21

Moles spend most of their lives
under the ground.

They dig tunnels looking for worms
to eat.

As they dig, they push soil up to
the surface.

This makes mounds called molehills.

Naked mole rats live in big groups. They hardly ever go above ground.

They dig tunnels using their big front teeth.

They smell out roots to eat.

Cassava root

23

Kingfishers live in burrows beside rivers.

A banded kingfisher dives into the river to catch fish.

Brook trout

She takes the fish back to her burrow and feeds it to her chicks.

Otters sleep in riverside burrows called holts.

They hunt for river creatures to eat.

Perch

They look after their pups in the holt too.

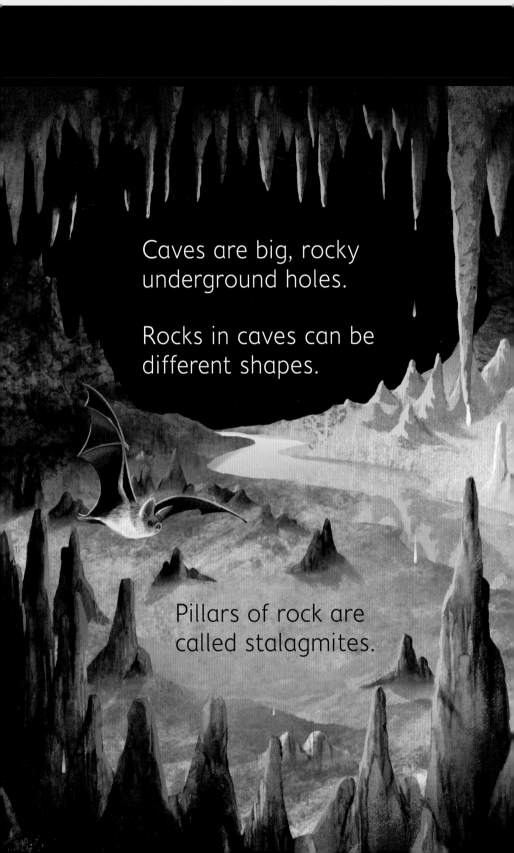

Caves are big, rocky underground holes.

Rocks in caves can be different shapes.

Pillars of rock are called stalagmites.

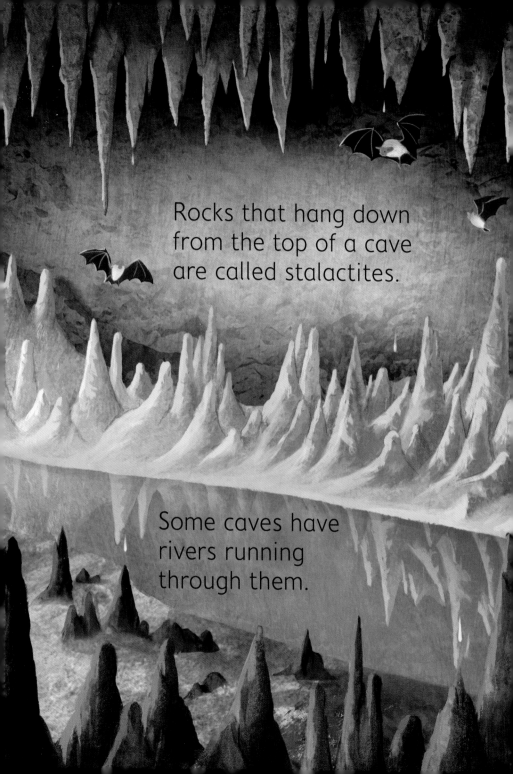

Rocks that hang down from the top of a cave are called stalactites.

Some caves have rivers running through them.

Unusual animals
live in dark,
underground caves.

Big brown bats sleep in caves.
They fly out at night to hunt for food.

Olms live in lakes deep inside caves.
They don't have any eyes.

Cave swallows build nests from
mud and bat droppings.

Cave spiders build sticky webs.
They eat bugs that get trapped.

Cricket

Grizzly bears sleep underground through the winter.

They catch lots of fish to eat at the end of summer.

Salmon

When a bear is going to have cubs,
she digs a den.

She takes in tree branches, leaves
and grass to line the den.

She gives birth to cubs. They grow
up in the den.

In spring, the mother and her cubs leave the den. They look for plants and animals to eat.

Digital retouching by John Russell

First published in 2018 by Usborne Publishing Ltd., Usborne House, 83-85 Saffron Hill, London EC1N 8RT England. www.usborne.com Copyright © 2018 Usborne Publishing Ltd. The name Usborne and the devices ♀ 🐝 are Trade Marks of Usborne Publishing Ltd. All rights reserved. First published in America 2018. UE.